DUNYAZAD

May Telmissany

DUNYAZAD

Translated from the Arabic and with a Postface by
Roger Allen

Saqi Books

This book has been translated and published with the assistance of the European Cultural Foundation within the framework of a programme launched simultaneously by editors in different European languages. Each of the retraced journeys in this series offers to European readers some Arab aspects of a shared heritage, the 'Mémoires de la Méditerrannée'.

The Programme currently includes the following languages: Catalan, Dutch, English, French, German, Italian, Polish, Spanish and Swedish.

British Library Cataloguing-in-Publication Data
A catalogue record for this book is available from the
British Library

ISBN 0 86356 340 6 (pb)
ISBN 0 86356 552 2 (hb)

First published in Arabic by
Dar Sharqyyat lil Nashr wal Tawzi', 1997

Saqi Books
26 Westbourne Grove
London W2 5RH

Contents

DUNYAZAD

Rose Basket

Dunyazad came to room 401 for the first and last time to say goodbye. She was wrapped in her tiny white shroud – several layers of clean muslin tied in three knots at head, feet, and waist, and a large sheet that made her little body look twice as large.

Her features poked eagerly through the cotton gauze. I asked the nurse to put the lights on, but the room was still dark. I stared down at the round, bluish face, the closed eyes, the tiny nose, and the pyramid-shaped mouth, now deep blue.

In spite of everything she had been alive, that serene face and tiny head now forsaken by life (and maybe soon to be erased by memory?). Just a few days ago it had burst from my womb into a world not yet ready to welcome it.

I uttered just one short phrase: she looked like me. Three

nurses stood around me, with my husband who hadn't seen her face before. Meaningless expressions of regret. One of the nurses kept stroking my hand and maybe my forehead as well. I wasn't wearing my glasses, so I was sorry I didn't notice them leave or look out of the window afterwards. My husband came back into the room, then left me again and departed with the crowd of people waiting outside. This time I burst into tears. She was so beautiful, I said; I couldn't call her by her name. Her name was not linked in any way to her tiny, lifeless body and to the smell of her which still pervaded the room.

That morning, Wednesday at nine or shortly after, I went out of room 401. I gestured to the nurse. 'I'm going to tell her now,' I said, 'so be ready.' I went back into the room. 'Everything's over,' I said to her, and we both cried. This time I really cried, something I had wanted to do when I was hugging her two days earlier, and I was afraid to. I gave the security man some money, and he quickly summoned his colleague. I got some more money out; I think it was twenty pounds. I went out with the three nurses in their blue uniforms; they looked a bit tense, as though they were feeling guilty. One of them carried the tiny shroud. We all hurried to the room where my wife was waiting for me. So everything was going as she wanted.

The sight of her serene little face gave me peace of mind

I hadn't felt for the past two days. For a few more moments I stared at her in the pale neon light, then they hurriedly covered her face again.

My wife's elder brother was waiting for us outside the door, standing there straight as the Sphinx, forlorn as a disused well. He may have been praying silently – only appropriate. I asked him to wait just a moment longer while I checked on her. Then we put the shroud into a basket I'd bought from a flower-seller nearby and covered it with roses. It looked like a tiny garden that had come instantly to full bloom (it was the very end of spring).

Dunyazad.

'We'll name her Dunyazad,' I told my mother, when I came round from the effects of the anaesthetic. 'Just as you wish, dear,' she replied, but she clearly didn't like that name. My husband was well aware that signing the death certificate would be the only time we would really get to name her. My brother was a believer in fate, but didn't want to remind me of the fact. Everyone kept on looking at me without saying a word.

I had woken up in pain at four o'clock on Monday morning. At first I paced around the house so as not to wake anyone up, then I tried going back to bed at six, and finally got up at eight. I told my husband. We dressed our only son even though he was still asleep and dropped him off at daycare; then we went to the bank and finally the hospital. They had me admitted. The doctor was as polite as usual.

Room 401 was clean. I undressed and started pacing back and forth to lessen the pain which was getting worse. I tried not to scream, but eventually I couldn't stop myself. My husband kept urging me to breathe normally. The assistant doctor came a number of times, and so did my own doctor. 'We'll wait,' they kept saying. But Dunyazad kept searching for a way out of her very first life-crisis. The doctor listened to the heartbeat dozens of times. For some reason he was worried, and I realized that something was going on.

In the end came the injection for the anaesthetic; that reduced the pain a bit, helped me make it through the final half-hour before being taken into the operating theatre (was the doctor delayed?). The room was not ready. I haemorrhaged three times, incredible effusions of blood and water. I was moved from one bed to another, and then to the operating table. I was aware of the anaesthetic wafting in through my nose. The head was already pushing out through the slit that the doctor had cut immediately. I was drowning in hot water. Everything dissolved in a haze; the final sense of white neon light, and one last thought: is it really . . . a girl?

Fifty minutes in the operating theatre now. I can't hear a sound. The absolute silence all around my seat keeps me isolated from the world. Over the door there's a notice illuminated by soft, red light: OPERATING THEATRE: NO ENTRY. Three doctors come up to me. She's fine. What about the baby? She died. I don't cry . . . I wait for more information. My brain starts pounding like a hammer. I see my wife coming out of the theatre, as though just to say goodbye. The protruding cheeks and dark circles under her eyes seem sure signs of imminent death.

Two hours with her in the room. The nurse keeps coming and going; she puts a glucose drip into the veins on each hand and taps lightly on her head. My wife opens her eyes and lets out a gentle sigh – I wonder what she's thinking about now. The skin is stretched tight over her cheekbones; those lovely eyes seem to be floundering in a desolate silence and her lips are colourless, their whiteness the hue of death.

I asked her two brothers to come . . . they were late . . . the younger one was the first to arrive. I told him the baby was stillborn . . . he cried and so did I. We'll tell her gradually, we said, just as the three doctors suggested. Then the elder brother arrived. We cried too. We agreed about other details as well. I can't remember what they were now, but I do know that I couldn't stay alone any longer. We all stood around the bed which held nothing

but her still baby. There was no way I could hold her in my
arms now, and perhaps not even tomorrow . . .

While I was hugging my husband early one morning, the
baby was kicking him, and he was laughing. Now the echo
of his laughter envelops me. I can feel my empty womb
moving in time with her breathing, even though her sweet
breath will never fill my nostrils like other children's. No
one ever let me see her breathing.

I had already bought Dunyazad a lovely, bright-coloured
crib covered in white tulle and lace. I had bought a lot of
other stuff as well, all of it packed away in drawers awaiting
her; all embroidered in rainbow colours and waiting: tiny
shoes, finger-sized socks that I'd put away in the hospital
suitcase a month or more ago. I wanted to dress her in some
of her own clothes rather than the normal burial shroud,
but, of course, they had to do their job properly.

I saw her twice on a small TV monitor divided into two:
first in the sixth month and again in the ninth: big head and
thigh bone. 'It's a girl,' the doctor told me in English. 'I'm
going to name her Zad,' I said, then my husband and I said
Dunyazad, just like the Thousand and One Nights. But she
spent just one night in hospital. Was it my lot to spend the
other thousand that lay ahead recalling a name that I only
ever got to say once, or maybe twice?

When the effects of the anaesthetic wore off and I

regained consciousness, it was to the sound of my husband's voice. I saw my mother's face. A subdued light filtered into the room from the bathroom. 'It's a girl,' they told me, 'she's very jaundiced.' So she's in the incubator. I can't see her now, I'll have to wait. 'She wasn't getting enough oxygen to the brain,' they went on. They said they were doing their best. Next morning it was: 'If she doesn't die, she'll be retarded. She's sleeping peacefully. Once in a while she convulses, and a white liquid oozes from her tiny mouth.' 'Her mouth looks like a triangle,' my brother remarked. A bit later my other brother said: 'God have mercy on her!' I did not believe it. All I could think of was that jaundice wasn't a life-threatening illness; at least, that's what I thought. So give her brain some oxygen and let her get up so that I can breastfeed her. I didn't believe it. My husband looked utterly miserable; everyone showed me the same voiceless sympathy (whose full import I only now understand); and yet I still didn't believe any of it.

Tuesday morning. I phoned my mother. We said, Let's go now and get the grave ready. I recall the last story my wife wrote. It begins: 'We've bought a grave.' At that point we hadn't even bought it. We went together to the family grave. On the way my mother did not cry, but she said a lot of things that I can't remember now. I was so tired, going over various picky details in my mind: the things I was telling my wife every day, how the baby was, all the time fully aware that since yesterday she had been in the hospital morgue.

I told myself: this evening I'll break it to her that the baby died in the incubator for lack of oxygen. Tomorrow morning would be best, the doctor had said. I ate something and so did my wife. She kept sending everyone to the nursery to check on the baby. Everyone was going out into the corridor and waiting by the window.

In the evening I wanted her to get some sleep. And ever so slowly it came.

Later I discovered that a noise in the corridor had woken her up.

In spite of everything I managed to get some sleep on Tuesday evening, a couple of hours. I woke up, had a cry, then went back to sleep. The doctor had given me a prescription to take at mealtimes; later I found out that it dries up breast milk.

After a couple of naps I woke up to the fourth-floor corridor filled with the sounds of a new birth. The doctor was congratulating everyone on the beautiful baby; we'll bring it to the mother in an hour, he said. The sounds in the corridor were all a jumble, but I could make out some of the voices: the father, a little boy jealous of his newborn sister, and the night nurse. There was a lot of laughter too. Next door all was happiness and joy, but in our room there was total silence. My husband was asleep, and a hazy image of Dunyazad, whom I had not even seen yet, inscribed itself on the room's space.

A sunny Wednesday morning. We opened the window and the sound of birds came bursting in. We packed our suitcases to leave. I asked my husband to check on Dunyazad. He cautioned me that by now she might be dead. We agreed that in spite of everything I should still see her. I said I would rather she died than live in unbearable pain. I was only trying to reassure him; I just wanted that tiny head of hers to be given a supply of oxygen and returned to its natural state. I waited for him to bring her to me in her embroidered white dress. I smiled and found self-assurance in my inner feelings and the gentle breeze wafting in through the window. 'A lovely, sunny day; no one can die today.'

The doctor's report noted that death had occurred inside the womb due to a total rupture of the placenta. I put the report into my pocket and went to the local health office. I got a burial licence, then hurried back. As usual she was waiting for me. The curtains were closed, and the room was shrouded in her silence. Everyone was waiting outside room 401, occasionally exchanging snippets of conversation. No name for the baby was recorded on the documents, so I couldn't say her name, something I'd wanted to do for years.

'Zad al-Rimal' (food of the sands), she whom my eyes had yet to see.

I remember my wife going to see the sonar specialist twice. I didn't go with her; now I can't recall why. Shehab al-Din went with her and saw a set of jumbled images that he proceeded to arrange in his young mind. He loved her, it seems, without even knowing it or realizing that now he was an only child again.

My husband left the room. I looked towards the window, waiting and listening apprehensively. He came back alone and sat on the edge of the bed. It's all over, he said, and hugged me. I stifled my screams. So the day had lied to me; so had the sun and birds. This wasn't a lovely day. Everyone said: you would have died for sure; it was a sudden haemorrhage; another half-hour in the operating theatre, and there would have been the risk of gangrene; blood-pouches dangling by my bed, glucose, and an intravenous needle. I can't believe it. The pain recedes, the danger symptoms diminish, and still there's the wait for the baby girl. In spite of everything she arrived, and my womb was never her grave.

After a while three nurses came in with a tiny white bundle; everything was absolutely discreet. We shouldn't defile a body once it's been wrapped in a shroud. 'Don't scream,' my husband warned me. I wanted to hold her in my arms, but they refused and took her away without my even realizing it. One of the nurses stayed with me, but I asked her to leave me alone. I told her I was fine.

She was fine when I left her. There was no screaming in the room. I didn't let her hold the tiny shroud. I wanted to do it myself, but I didn't. We hurried. My mind was drilled for what had to be done. We drove calmly to the graveyard in my elder brother's car; I sat beside him, and the basket of roses was on the back seat beside my mother. A tiny procession with no one but us. I wondered what the youngsters would do when we got to the graveyard, and panicked as I contemplated what might happen to interfere with our task.

An eerie quiet. The graveyard was empty, and the winding road seemed burdened by the end of a hot spring. The shroud was lowered on its own, and the basket of roses was left for the small children.

My husband's mother arrived, then my own mother. We got

everything ready to leave the hospital. Two days out of life; the spectre of inexorable death infiltrates the very pores of the room.

At the main door of the hospital I spotted the security man in his blue uniform. Two days ago he'd smiled at me as I'd been walking round and round the hospital vestibule trying to rid myself of the constant pain.

I huddle up on my own in the waiting car. Four years ago, I remember, I was holding my first child. The sun was shining in through the window. As he lay there in my arms, I was overcome by a childish sense of exultation. But this time those arms are empty. My womb feels its loss, and I am left to agonize over the gaping wound and emptiness inside me. As we head for home, everything is silence.

I drink a bottle of juice, lean back on a small pillow, and try to get some sleep in the car. We take our son home too; he had come with his grandmother and was settled in the front seat. 'Shehab's baby sister has gone back into Mummy's tummy,' he said with all the conviction of his four years, 'so she can get bigger.' Then he added: 'Get well, Mummy dear!'

As we drove home I told myself I'd give her all the details when the time was right. I bought plenty of cartons of juice and a few other things. I began to wonder when our daughter had actually been born and when she'd died.

According to my wife, Dunyazad was born at approx-
imately three thirty in the afternoon on 15 May 1995 and
died on 16 May in the evening. She also said, 'my womb
wasn't her grave for a single day,' but I knew otherwise.

On the way home I turned towards her and gave her a
pat on the legs. That dreadful question kept pounding
away: when was our daughter really born, the one I'd
watched a few hours earlier being lowered into an under-
ground vault?

Bed was a refuge from my mother's frowns. I didn't even
bother to take my clothes off, but fell into a deep sleep.
When I woke up, the scar was still aching a lot. A jumbled
pile of questions kept flashing through my mind, then
quickly evaporating. I heard voices outside the room. I
undressed slowly and asked my mother to go home. She was
very put out, but did as I asked. Now it was just us, my
husband and I, and Shehab al-Din (who was his usual sweet
little self), each of us trying desperately to avoid looking at
the other and suppressing an overwhelming desire to scream
out loud.

My husband isn't thinking about it. He's busy preparing
meals, dealing with medicine times, and responding to the
little boy's needs. He has kept his sorrows bottled up inside
him; given time, their impact quickly recedes. We have
decided not to receive anyone at home; friends start crying,

and acquaintances use the occasion to share our tears. So we spend the first week on our own. My mother arrived nevertheless with food and some fresh stories. She was glad to see me safely recovered. I'm the daughter she brought into the world (but what about my own daughter?); she pushes me right to the brink of madness. My younger brother came too, bringing roses and a great deal of love, the way I've always remembered him. He didn't stay long. Two days later he was back again to put a breach in our cordon of isolation. Then my friend Nora arrived; at first I refused to see her, but, when she came again, I greeted her with a re-assuring smile. We chatted a lot. With my mind wandering I asked about her own eight-month-old daughter. I can remember the day she was born (I wonder, was my daughter really born?), when I held her in my arms for the first time. After that lots of other friends came to visit; by then time had passed, and I could look them in the eye without inevitably thinking back.

I count days without using numbers; instead I use the ever-growing interval between them and Monday 15 May. Then comes the evening when I find some scraps of paper on which my husband noted down the hospital reports, the number of blood transfusions, various expenditures, the times I had gone into and come out of the operating theatre, and the text of the doctor's report that resulted in the issuance of the burial certificate. There it is in black and white: 'Death occurred inside the womb due to a total rupture of the placenta.'

With that I broke down and cried as never before. So she had never lived outside her womb–grave. They had all lied to me. I had believed them because I wanted her to have lived for at least a single day; in my own memory I could turn that short space of time into years. She had emerged from my womb–grave to be placed into her own grave; all she left behind was the memory of a bluish face that I can see in the colour of the morning sky and in the crumpled bed-covers beside me as evening falls – the face of a sleeper, stifled, yet beautiful.

I'd planned to tell you when you got better, was my husband's reply.

But I was still not feeling any better. My mind went on functioning like clockwork; images came flashing back one after another, occupying different spaces inside my head. I started going over what had happened and asking my husband who knew about it; all the people who came to visit and didn't ask about her; all the baby gifts that were never delivered. They all stared in alarm at my smiling face. On the table were bottles of perfume and a profusion of roses; house plants in the corners of the room (that were not decorating my daughter's grave).

When my wife came out of the operating theatre, I was convinced I would lose her. When my baby daughter left the hospital in a basket of roses, the sense of loss was fully confirmed. Two images have implanted themselves like thorns in my heart: my wife's face and the tranquil features of my daughter; they both confront me constantly. I'll write a poem about her, I told myself, but I never did. How can I preserve that moment or even recall it when I feel so scared and helpless? For years I've been practising self-control. Every moment imposes its particular grief on the memory and carves its own winding paths inside the head. Should you wish to recall it, back it will come. (But do I really want to?)

When my friend Amina came to visit, my wife wept in her arms and then in her husband's arms. I was feeling a childish need for friends and family, even a few miscellaneous acquaintances. It was a genuine need; I wanted someone to pat my hand and wipe death's images from my brow, images so close, so plausible, so all-encompassing. 'Why aren't you crying?' my wife kept asking me incredulously and then she said, 'maybe I don't really know you yet.'

I recollect the initial moments of pain like an oyster. I discover I've forgotten the taste, shape, and smell of pain.

All that remains is a desire to reshape the world according to the laws of what is not there.

Now I have returned to my husband, my only son, my only house, and a few friends. But I have yet to find my own self, something I thought I knew. I'd often felt we were a family of four, but I could only locate three of them. For nine months I'd been preparing to welcome into our midst that fourth person who was growing inside me with all those daily details.

Today I miss that person and have to pick up my life as it was before. My body has resumed its normal behaviour, and everything has gone back to square one.

Even so I am determined not to forget; on every possible occasion I name things once more. So she was Dunyazad, but from today she'll only ever be those few lines on a page. Now I recall the image of her when for the first time I saw her thigh on the screen in the doctor's clinic, the screen they use to measure the embryo's age; and then the second time, with the cluster of dots for measuring how long she was. Everything was just as it should have been. I can remember other things too, many things I haven't said. Now my nipples hang down uselessly. When I undress, I turn away from the mirror.

Morning Newspaper

Being shocked by a smiling face you recognize isn't easy. It's a sunny morning, and you're standing by the window. You read the name on the obituary page edged in black. You stare at the buildings in the distance, searching for a memory, a picture like the smiling face in that photograph; the facial muscles seem to be moving, as though to say 'This face was alive.'

You bumped into him just a few days ago in a corridor and exchanged a rapid greeting. 'Let's call each other,' you said, but nothing came of it because you killed the opportunity then and there and forgot about it.

To have that happen to me now isn't easy. After losing Dunyazad, I discovered that grief is like a thread that stretches from throat to heart, ploughing a rough furrow as it goes; its length is scored by images of pain while the sides remain rigid. Time passes. Every time I feel my neck, I realize the trench is still there; with each new strand of pain, cracks are filled and the agony gets worse.

It's a hot summer day. Dunyazad is long gone. Since her death I've taken to perusing the obituaries on the last-but-one page of the morning papers. This is what happened to me. Right in the middle of the smiling face in the obituary photograph, underneath the printed letters and between the lines of the lengthy text, her face suddenly loomed, mingled with all the blood of labour and the bluish hue of that death that would not be delayed. Two minutes, and then I touched the surface of that face. I folded up the newspaper and decided not to mark this occasion with tears. Had he died too? That way?

The picture: a man in his fifties, maybe sixties, with a beard and round spectacle frames. The scent of aftershave wafts from the pores of his face with their velvet touch. A gentle smile; teeth out of sight but nicely regular, leaving just a tiny space for his tongue-tip as a child. Cheeks prominent like the sculpture of an aged fisherman; tiny eyes behind the glasses that reflect light on to the left cheek; a slight stoop in the shoulders.

The chest continues under the picture, then the waist and legs; the ensemble reaches completion at the bottom of the page. The obituary takes up a whole column too. The picture is immobile, but it looks like drawings of the Pharaohs of old, ready for movement and fixed in the memory.

I know tales of him like the old fables about genies and gremlins. On noisy evenings his stories scare me. When I'm on my own I remember some of the details, and I smile.

A few days ago he ran into me in one of the corridors and told me a brief story, then we quickly said our goodbyes. We have to get together, we said, some time soon.

The story: imagine. My wife came home from work at three in the afternoon. She was in pain; her left leg was still hurting from the effects of an old fracture. I made her lie down on the wooden bed and put a pillow under her leg. Standing alone in the kitchen, I noticed cracks in the wall. I drank a whole bottle of mineral water in one swallow, but it didn't get me drunk!

Now the wife is crying; she's staring at the smiling face in the morning paper. The pain in her left leg is getting worse. One wall is leaning towards another. The bottles of non-intoxicating mineral water are all lined up properly in their never-emptying box.

Just before noon. A hot breeze is blowing in through a small aperture in the window. The newspaper pages rustle and make you feel drowsy; caught by the breeze, they stir a little and flutter like wings of tiny birds. For a moment they settle back on each other, but then the warm breeze lifts them again. They provide a brief glimpse of that smiling face, just a beard and half a mouth. Once in a while I spot it and touch my face where he hurriedly planted a farewell kiss that day. I close my eyes and surrender to a counter-breeze coming from the door. Behind closed eyelids I see the sun setting, throwing its shadow across my room.

I hear the sound of shoeless feet, bare feet on polished tiles and feel myself enveloped by the noise they make as they touch the soft surface. When I reopen my eyes, there I see – standing right in front of me – myself as a little girl less than three years old, tiny, thin, with a smile like the sun. I give myself a hug and kiss and call myself Dunyazad, who looked so much like me.

Again I close my eyes, and my child image recedes. In its place comes his smiling picture. This time it is the sound of military boots, the clanking of prison doors, and whips hung over people's heads. Rapidly I erase the smiling picture from the eye's memory; I look round in alarm at all four corners of the room. The newspaper is still on the table, the breeze is still warm, and a softer flow wafts in through the open door. I relax back into my chair, stretch my legs out on the table, and soon doze off.

Dream: Dunyazad is three weeks old today. I light a candle for her and carry it to her silent tomb in a corner of the room. I open the grave-door and sidle my way in to where the tiny body lies. Placing the candle beside her, I burst into tears. In a secret ritual of love I see her plant a warm kiss on my forehead, warm as the closed grave itself. The candle flickers and melts, making a fresh circle of wax alongside the others.

When at last I shut the door on her, I find myself searching for somewhere else in the room that would be fit for a grave for the person in the picture.

I start constructing a funerary mastaba like the ones for Pharaohs. I try to remember the proportions of the body soon to be buried inside it.

Now the wife stops crying. She can feel a hollow space in the bed, one he was filling that evening . . . he said he'd take a short nap because he had to meet someone. He moved twice before finally settling on the left side. Night-time came. When the wife tried to wake him up, she had forgotten which meeting he'd been talking about.

It's happening to me.

Losing a friend without even shedding a tear. Death is an unfulfilled rendezvous between us, a fresh grave in my room.

A New Dress for the Occasion

Monday evening again; the same old round, day after day.

'You should go back to work now,' Nora remarked with a yawn.

Nora is my young friend. I like her a lot; I have yet to bury her in a secret vault in my heart. She stopped yawning. 'What am I going to do without you?' she asked in a tone of voice I recognized. Nora was the friend I sometimes went to work with; we always gossiped about other people. That's how I came to cut short my phone conversation with Nora and found myself knocking on her door; in my hand was an envelope containing my letter of resignation. I had written just two short words. 'You'll be fine,' I replied as Nora's face appeared behind the door.

I was asleep. In my complicated dreams I saw my friend's

face receding, edging towards a distant corner of the room (the one I'd painted black, closing the window on my solitude). I must have talked in my sleep. I woke to the sound of her voice on the phone: 'I'm coming by in ten minutes. You're the only one who can submit my resignation for me.' I tried to focus on the words, but they refused to conform. 'No argument,' she went on, 'I'm coming by now. This is it, Nora.'

My name's Nora. It took me a while to realize what was happening, but then I got ready to welcome her. That morning – a bright Monday morning – the boss telephoned. He was fuming. 'Your friend's slacking on the job,' he said. 'I'm going to take all necessary steps against her!' The room was full of junior employees. I realized the whole thing was a melodrama.

I sat on the small chair I normally sat on when visiting. Putting the envelope down on the edge of the wooden table, I looked up at her and smiled. She brought me a glass of chilled water and sat down beside me. Then she relayed to me the conversation she had had with our boss, how she had tried to explain that his time estimates were wrong.

My memory took me swiftly back to room 401. I envisioned myself getting slowly out of bed, staring at the bathroom door as if in some remote dream, and then collapsing on the clean floor.

Touching the floor sent a charge through me. I leapt to my feet. I felt a bit unsteady and asked Nora for another glass of water. 'Now you'll feel fine,' Nora said. 'Let's go,' was all I said in reply.

Our street is clean. In the evening cars are parked on both sides, and a breeze blows down the entire length. Neither of us said a word, we just walked side by side. I felt like kissing her between the eyes, but didn't. She wasn't so much sad as angry. I really wanted her to vent her anger at anything, at people's resigned expressions, at the treeless winding street, or even at me. After today, I told myself, I won't be seeing as much of her as before. 'How about going to the movies next Thursday,' I suggested. 'I'll give you a call if anything changes,' she replied. So we agreed to meet, then each of us went her own way. Her husband was waiting for her. Her tiny house was overflowing with books and night-time discussions, but I knew nothing about all that.

I went home alone and let the door slam hard. I remembered a story my friend had written a few months back, called 'Resignation'.

Once I had made my way through the oppressive breeze to the front door of our house, I suddenly remembered a story I'd written a few months back called 'Resignation'. Once the tension of the first few moments was over, I told my husband what had happened, and he gave me a hug. Then he went to his room to think.

Almost as though I were dreaming I pictured my work colleagues as dinosaurs from ancient times, complete with tails and small heads. I actually felt my own backside just to make sure I wasn't growing a prehistoric tail again.

I felt completely at ease with my decision to reject any compromise. 'Tomorrow I'll go in person,' I told myself. 'I'm not afraid of confrontations.'

Important papers in various colours spread out on the long conference table. The wood panelling in the room has changed colour. The large desk by the front wall gleams in the sunlight coming in through the closed window. Conditioned air comes out of the metal box, soundless and odourless. I float across the void between door and desk, passing the long table. I manage to get by other small obstacles too and to overcome my general sense of boredom. I put a single faded document on the desk, not even looking at the short man who remains seated in his raised chair. We exchange a few words before he writes his signature below mine. I become aware of the breeze wafting over my head, but find no trace of my naked picture.

That night I read the paragraph from the story again. But this time I write a real resignation. No need to open an inquiry. 'I request, Sir, that you consent to my resignation,' followed by 'Please accept . . .' That way there'll be no implications beyond what's clear from the basic facts. No other wording is appropriate. A lot of respect, concision, and careful planning. On the new envelope I write the boss's name and underline it to bring everything to closure.

I craft a series of mental pictures of the next day's meeting. Eventually I decide to say nothing at all. That's how I started constructing a new cemetery where I could put a statue of the man and cover it with earth. I remember that when Dunyazad died, he sent me a letter: 'You'll be born again amid cascades of pain.' At that point I was still spending a lot of time every day weeping for Dunyazad (so what has changed in the meantime?).

On Tuesday morning I spent half the time still asleep, and the other half in the office. As the time passed, I was storing in my mind images of the place and the people going to and fro. Every time their eyes met, there was whispered conversation about me.

The office manager is a decent man. He looked scared as he took my resignation. 'I'll see him in his office to submit it in person,' I told him. He signed an acknowledgement of the letter's receipt, while all the employees clustered around and behind the doors. Then a half-hour wait, an age that I spent reading some documents I'd brought with me specifically to pass the time.

I remembered Nora's face from last night as she tried to stop me leaving.

The phone didn't ring on Tuesday morning as I'd anticipated. I was expecting her to change her mind, but she didn't.

I got my daughter's breakfast ready, put it on the kitchen table, and waited.

I didn't have long to wait. He arrived. 'The office manager has a copy,' I said, placing in front of him the only document feasible in the circumstances. He didn't say a word. I turned and headed for the door. A light breeze blew in from the window opposite, and I heard the sound of papers flying. I closed the office door. 'From today,' I told myself, 'I'll never hear that sound again. I'll never cross these thresholds, maybe for years to come.' The secretary smiled at me. 'That quick?' she asked. Over her head there loomed a large question mark.

I crossed the street to look in a shop window; I liked the look of a brightly coloured dress. I hesitated for just a moment, but then made my mind up and went in. This 'first act' after

Dunyazad's death would mean some lean months, but the occasion still called for celebration.

It Was a House in the Fields

Arguments in the next room. Smoke, the smell of cigarettes, voices, muffled movements, doors slamming, opened windows, chairs being pushed across the polished wooden floor. 'We're going to sell the house,' said the uncle, and so did his daughter, and the mother, not to mention the crafty lawyer who was expecting to make sixty thousand Egyptian pounds. My husband said he was very fond of the street that had now been sold off by the people who lived there; he was very fond of the house as well. 'And now,' he went on, 'we're going to sell just like everyone else.' In the quiet of the adjoining room I recalled how five years ago I'd come here in a white dress; now it was hanging mute in the closet, wrapped in a dust-covered plastic bag. My husband had picked me up and carried me over a huge trench in front of the door. The neighbours were tearing their house down and having trenches dug for water pipes and drains for a new twelve-storey building. He carried me through the iron gate and over wooden planking made specially for us. We celebrated our joyous wedding night to the sound of bulldozers. At that point I thought about calling the police; earth diggers pounding away in my ears and the uncle's gruff voice too. The police aren't at anyone's service.

Amid all this sudden din I hear her in the room next door. She's sitting in her chair with a view of the back garden, breathing quietly and waiting impatiently for everyone to leave. For a moment I stare at the lawyer with his bushy moustache; in his prominent cheekbones I detect the features of my old grandfather. Thirty years ago he had used my grandmother's money and the value of the agricultural property far away to build the house. My grandfather had housed all his sons there, married them off, and watched as their children padded across the grass in the back garden. There he was, still staring down at me from the window on the ground floor. When my uncle took the photograph, I was wearing short trousers and smiling up at him from my tricycle. I kept it in my box till we got married and had a son. But he can't pad around on the grass in the back garden because we're renting it out to entrepreneur builders. And today we're going to sell the house; we'll have pictures of it to keep in our boxes and

*two million Egyptian pounds in our bank accounts. The
lawyer began to stare at me till our eyes melted into silence
that unravelled . . . suddenly.*

'Two million,' my husband proposed unequivocally. 'The
land's not worth any more than that,' the buyer
commented, 'and, as you well know, that is without
permits . . . and demolition costs, not to mention other
expenses I can't afford.' 'Agreed,' replied Uncle in a gruff,
scratchy voice. He wanted to exclude my husband from the
bargaining process and close the deal as quickly as possible.
Mother was furious. She left the room and came into mine
looking for something or other, she didn't know what. I
didn't say a word. Instead I set about rubbing the little one's
back; he was standing next to me by the window. At this
point Dunyazad would have been screaming her head off; I
would have cuddled her and turned her face towards the
sky. By now she would be in her third month; she'd weigh
over eight kilograms. I would be putting her down for a nap
in her tiny bed. Isn't it time everyone left?

*By now she'll be waiting for my answer. If I agree to the
terms of sale, she'll say: He gave in to Uncle. When I object
to the price, she says: Let's get it over! When I say nothing,
the response is: He always hesitates. From the room next
door come her reactions to my imagined actions. I can't*

think any more. I leap up from my chair and silently head towards the closest window. I pretend to be thinking things over, but all I can see is the old photograph of my grandfather, and my wife's drawing. I am thinking about anything other than the price being offered for the house. Two million! A totally meaningless figure, exciting, yet meaningless. What can anyone buy with money like that?

A new house I'm dreaming about: domes, curves, antique wooden doors, a small garden, and a white porcelain pool; a house where Dunyazad can crawl fearlessly wherever she wants. It too fades in the memory, just like the picture of her in that firmly locked tomb. Now instead of that dream house we have a small flat somewhere or other in the world; it serves for the three of us, my husband, myself, and Shehab al-Din.

Three new houses we're buying. In the capital, one for my mother, another for us. In our summer place there's a house for winter and summer vacations. We've exchanged the one big house for three small ones; in so doing we've forever erased Grandfather's name that was inscribed over the outside door of the old house. Now I imagine pickaxes closing in on my nose, and I recoil with a start. Turning to the lawyer with the moustache, I suggest a compromise to

*resolve the issue. Everyone welcomes the idea, and at last
things are settled.*

Now boxes of various shapes will start piling up by the
entrance to the old house, underneath a tree whose
branches withered and died not long ago, a solitary mango
tree in the small yard that looks out on to the narrow street.
A removals van will come to take our heavy boxes away,
separate piles with their different colours and identities;
boxes with thirty years of my husband's memories, and my
own boxes from just the past five years, small and cosy. It's
almost as though they contain the kittens of a sick cat that
dies soon afterwards, leaving them orphans – tiny, cuddly,
and cute; like Shehab al-Din's four years and the not yet
three months of Dunyazad.

> *I told my wife we were going to sell the house. Imprinted
> on my mind were pictures of Dunyazad who had never
> seen a day like this, of my grandmother, and my younger
> uncle who died a martyr. I also recalled my grandfather
> who had taught me to read sitting in a wicker chair under
> the vine trellis; after a while it had been turned into a
> cement garage.*
>
> *All these boxes will get piled into the removals van and
> taken somewhere I know. No time for dreams now.
> They're all going somewhere I know.*

The house walls with their changed colour. The old stove in the kitchen. White tiles covering the wall's lower half, then yellow up to the ceiling. The small bathroom with its blue mosaic; the large one with its special aroma and white window looking out on the fields of old where reeds have been turned into cement blocks and leaves are now dark-brown metal sheets. The green fields of old are now buried under blocks of flats, shops, supermarkets, and paved roads. I came here just five years ago. Through my husband's eyes I saw the dry canals and water-wheels, the wide streets and coloured bicycles ridden by friends. Doqqi Square loomed on the horizon, with its statue of Saʿd Zaghloul, and beyond it the Nile – it all seemed like paintings of the middle ages.

We're selling the house. Tomorrow the first axe-blow will strike the wooden tiles on the top floor. The inevitable arrival of the demolition contractor, just as with all the other houses on the street. The mechanical digger that greeted my husband and me on our wedding night will pound again, but this time it will be inside the heads of two other newlyweds in an air-conditioned room in one of those flats on the twelfth floor. But they won't hear the noise of the digger or the air-conditioner; they won't call the police after midnight. There's no longer a law against noise at night.

The land's worth more than two million Egyptian pounds. The flat we're moving to is ready for us. Our old boxes sit there by the door. Before long we'll make space for new ones that can be dispersed to every single corner of the new house and extend their roots as far as our neighbour's roof. They'll enable us to keep alive those night-time conversations where we chat about old houses that change colour.

The Game of Death

A huge square, white sheet. Four men, maybe more, holding on to the edges. They toss you in the air, then with a great yell catch you again. Your eyes can't focus, and you're out of breath. Your heart almost loses its moorings every time you approach a peak that feels so remote even though you're standing on your own two feet. Your mind is racing: when's the game of death going to end? When it's all over, will your gait look peculiar? (Have you ever read the *Lucky Luke* comic-book stories?)

A barrel full of oil or tar. A group of strong cowboy kids stands jeering around you, the new outsider just arrived in their town remote in the desert. Right by the huge barrel they toss you in the white sheet, then dip you in the oil for a moment before shoving you into a huge pile of white chicken feathers that stick all over you. You still feel sick and startled. Looking like a huge cock covered with feathers, you feel utterly miserable (can you still remember the children's comic-books?).

You wash in the hotel nearby to rid yourself of the stench of black oil and the sheer shock of it all. Standing solidly on your feet, you button up your brown jacket. Suppressing a desire to vomit you step out into the desert and savour your victory. Some of the boys spot you and head in your direction; others scoff at your English reserve. But by now you have learned about the game of death; you know all the tests involved in their hazing rituals by heart. You've become a real man. Now you can smoke a rolled cigarette and deliberately let it dangle to the right from your lip. Yes indeed, insert your hand in the slim waistcoat pocket, stare off into the distance, and look pensive. Now you're Lucky Luke himself. All you need is a good, lean horse, that can join you in your silence, deep thoughts, adventure, and loneliness. Now you can lord it over those stupid wretches; you're their master. No one can tie your hands and feet to four pegs in the desert sun and pour honey all over you so ants can have a feast; no one can lead you to a narrow defile between two mountains just to pour boiling oil on you and your horse; none of them will dare annoy you while you're drinking liquor in the only saloon in town, packed full of idiots. Beyond all that, you can grab your girl around the waist, the one in the red dress with shiny-black embroidery, and kiss her on the mouth in full view of everyone. They all envy you, but none of them dares even come near her while you're away. You can leave the hotel without paying the bill or needing a friend as escort. You'll be back, back on the same old page in the same old comic-book, *The Game of Death*.

Maybe that's not the word for it in French. I read the *Lucky Luke* stories when I was twelve. I can still remember the details of the game; one evening recently they all came flooding back. I was counting days in the fourth month after Dunyazad's death: nine, and it was Thursday. Monday no longer brought its own special brand of sorrow, and the fifteenth of the month no longer left a lump in my throat. But I was still crying.

Perhaps I've really embarked on a similar death game of my own, involving some other initiation ritual that kills fear and the shock impact. Then all that remains is to acquire an immunity to loss, a resigned fatalism, and a sense of anticipation; it's like sipping unsugared tea every day without getting the sour taste. So again, all that remains is to orchestrate another night of lovemaking like the one I recall almost a year ago and create yet another dream – by waiting. I wonder, will it be a girl this time? What will I call her?

When you think about death every single day, it's not easy to get out of the rut. You land up losing a few atoms of your tangible existence. As days go serenely by, strands of hair may fall to the floor; at night insomnia may leave you lying wide awake in bed. You chew the ends of your fingernails while reading the morning newspaper; you may not feel much like eating either, and that means you'll lose a few extra kilograms. For the first time in your life you have to wear spectacles, and every day after lunch you take two pills prescribed by the doctor. Your legs feel shaky, so at night you use a large pillow to keep them elevated. After your usual nightmare you sit up in bed, and blood rushes to your head; you stagger to the bathroom and throw up. Food, medicine, and the will to stay alive, they all make you sick. But by now you're familiar with the game of death. So no tricks this time; no rushing again to be tossed in that white sheet that lifts you to the tree-tops and then pulls you down again, eyes rolling. Just look at your lovely pale complexion in the bathroom mirror and remember that you're still alive.

Once the bleeding stopped, I waited five days. I lit a candle in our square-shaped bedroom and put on a translucent white nightie which I left wide open at the top so my neck and breasts were visible. I lay down beside my husband and started watching the shadow patterns on the bed and cupboard. Everything in the room yielded to the dancing light from the red candle, bouncing on the walls slowly and in endless repetition (and you, my friend, keep tumbling into your white sheet and then almost immediately soaring up into the air again between their heads and the tree-tops close by; up, down, then up again, all the while thinking you will never touch ground again, then up and up and up to the tune of their frenzied shouts, till there comes that one last moment when you plunge to the ground just in time to grab the edge of the now motionless sheet. Amid all their cackling and banter you can hear your heart pounding and manage to rub your eyes. You are still alive, waiting for the next ordeal).

My husband gave me a gentle push. I was spreadeagled naked on top of him. Beads of sweat covered our chests. I rolled over on to my back beside him and ran my hand over my stomach; it felt scrunched up inside me as though cowering in fear. So what's this game we're playing again?

You're challenging your own fear; that's all there is to it. You're listening to the sound of blood pulsing hot through your veins and doing up your jacket buttons again so that you won't be affected by wind coming in through the summer window. You're thinking about your lean horse, your girlfriend who is so infatuated with you, and your desert stretching away to infinity. Oblivious to everything, you proceed along the path you have drawn with your own hand on the page of the sky. Death came, then left. Waiting is pointless.

A Nagging Question Early in the Morning

Early morning. The road from Giza to the south is always busy. A patch of light from my window shines down on the al-Marbutiya Canal. When . . .

For a while I just stared at the ceiling. Suddenly I realized that from now I'd never be writing about death; I'd only ever remember Dunyazad by her name. Now I compute the interval between two points; I'm aware that months have passed, more than four at any rate.

'So has the wound finally healed?' my friend asked me today. I don't know which of the two he's talking about. 'Yes,' I reply. There's the doctor as well, who's assured me I can have more children. They won't die . . . maybe . . . Or has the wound not really healed?

So I severed the bonds caused by these anxieties and spent a night of love in my husband's arms.

He buries half his head in the opposite wall and half his back in mine. A night of love that hasn't borne fruit as yet, but we're waiting. Confirmation won't put an end to doubt . . .

I begged this friend not to ask me about my wound again.

A moment of slow detachment from the past. I use wood planks to prevent my heart from collapsing. I tug strands of love from one aperture to another, from throat to womb. Why do I feel that lump in my throat every time I think I was 'a grave' for her?

I close my womb to the blood of my next period; I want it to come in spite of everything.

I write about waiting, about the awesome truth of there being another creature inside me, growing amid familiar capillaries that enfold traces of spermatozoa resembling us.

Or I write about a failing memory that still preserves a bluish face on the surface of a blue sky and now occupies 'heaven's' place. So where is 'the master of the throne'? How many kilometres separate him from Dunyazad's tiny round face?

Or I write about the way one kind of fear can overpower

another. Like worrying about getting your clothes dirty when you're standing in a crowd of utterly chic and pointless people; or being scared of your own image on the television when the announcer asks you what you meant by the title *Repetitive Sculptures*. You read the newspapers every day in case they forget to mention your name on the literary page. You call a family friend to make sure her children are well and that she saw you on television last night.

Or I write about alternative solutions, other loves, another adventure beside that of creation. It's like throwing yourself into the clutches of a comedy and convincing yourself to laugh amid the shallowness of its deadbeat characters; or scoffing at an old man, kidding him that he can still hold a cane to cross a street just twenty metres wide; or playing the game of a mature woman unruffled at being over thirty who can now unbutton her shirt without shame.

I can write about anything now, except death. I've forgotten the number of days. A white cloud has passed over the surface of that bluish face in its clear, blue sky over yonder. I've lured my husband into bed with a genuinely sluttish gesture so I can produce another baby that won't die. There we are: I am writing the word 'die'.

The road from Giza to the south goes past my window which looks out on the al-Marbutiya Canal. There's a second road that goes up to the small villages near Giza, where they make popular galabiyas and wool and silk prayer-rugs. There's another road too, a secret one that goes between two apertures, throat and womb; that's the one I have made to open up my stomach, traverse the obstacles of the body, and stretch threads between my sense of death and my being a woman who can give birth. At night's end one question always imposes itself . . . so . . .

A Window on Waiting

On the fourth-floor balcony. The road overlooking it is deserted. Ten in the morning. All is quiet. Closed windows, lots of them, and distant balconies glinting in the sunlight. There I stand upright, watching specks of dust landing on the balcony railing and gradually dulling its dark red paint. The children are all at school. The men's cars left resignedly by the pavement proclaim that their owners have no regular job; so in the morning, while the children are at school, they have sex with their wives, read the newspaper on the toilet, and smoke a single cigarette after breakfast. Behind all these windows and tightly shut doors, there's a sluggish daily traffic – from bedroom, to corridor, to bathroom, to kitchen. The salon is kept dark; the drawn curtains deprive the gleaming gold-leaf furniture of the light it craves. I glance over the balcony railing and notice the neighbours' washing hanging wet on coloured, plastic clotheslines. There's a faded blanket that's gone straight from hamper to full-automatic washing machine to fresh air; it's still heavy with water, giving a hint of winter's approach and the end of autumn. Then there are house-clothes for a baby who's not yet one, white, coloured, and dazzling Ariel-bright. They sway gently in the morning breeze. A few puffs of steam float up into the air and deposit invisible droplets on the red railing of my balcony where they mingle with the dust, airborne water blending with capricious dust particles. I never touch the balcony railing. Suddenly I yell for Umm Hani, who trudges her way out and stares at me like a mountain hawk. I ask her to give the balcony wall a good clean. I vanish into the dark interior, carrying a nasty stench in my nostrils, and in my ears the sound of a long piece of cloth against the railing removing accumulated dust and water.

So this is how daily images pile up in the recesses of my mind and the balcony plays its part in the Monday morning routine. Umm Hani comes to clean, and I go out on the balcony; otherwise I only go out there to hang up the washing or bring it back in. In a glance I take in the tree-lined street, the canal opposite, the surrounding buildings, drawn curtains, and neighbours' washing hung out on balconies near and far . . . In another glance the time has shifted to almost one in the afternoon. The muezzin has finished the noon call to prayer or else he's honing his gravelly voice to announce the start of the prayer itself . . . Dutiful housewives start stirring food in saucepans; some wonderful smells waft through the air, but others betray a genuine ignorance. Sounds of men in sweet slumber are audible, so women close the doors of their bedrooms. A bit later the gas under saucepans is lowered, women remove their dirty patterned aprons, put on large headscarves, go downstairs and head for the top of the street to wait for children coming home from school, huge multi-coloured buses arriving and leaving. The children jump up and down, asking what's for lunch today. The wives don't reply, just hurry home for lunch, then a nap.

I wasn't watching Umm Hani work today, so she's done everything quickly. She's standing by the entrance talking to the doorman for a bit before catching the minibus to Helwan. I know she counts the twenty pounds carefully going down the stairs; one pound she keeps in her hand, the rest she stuffs into her ample bosom where it disappears into two mounds of unfettered flesh. I only watch her as she crosses the street. I remind myself she'll be back soon, next Monday in fact. At eight-thirty in the morning I'm jolted awake by the doorbell; I'm still on the balcony at ten, and I only close the balcony doors at one when she leaves. At this point a delightful silence settles on the house. I draw the curtains, look at the tables, and run my hands over them.

There's no dust, but I'm still not satisfied; there are traces of the wet duster in the corners. I turn the light off and head for the bathroom where water courses over my exhausted body. I think of Shehab al-Din who'll soon be coming home with my husband. As soon as he gets home, I tell myself, I'll put him in the bath and run water over his head. The dirt from the school playground will still be stuck to his feet, but I'll give in to his blackmail and yelling and forget about the rest of his body. I dry myself after the hot bath (and I'll dry him too once he comes home). Lying down on the bed for a final half-hour's rest, I sense the emptiness on his side. Dunyazad would sleep quietly beside me; her rosy mouth would smile and a single tiny white tooth would be visible between her lips. I smile because she has begun her teething early; every so often she never fails to give me a wonderful smile, and that makes me happy.

My stomach does a little turn; by this time the baby must be lying in the hollow of my womb. As yet there is no mouth, nor any real body parts. It won't be long before I get to show off his white house-clothes to the neighbours when I exhibit them on the front part of the clothesline. When Umm Hani comes on Monday mornings I won't have to escape to the balcony; in fact I'll spend the whole time with him in his sunlit room, playing with his big nose and soft hands. My hand sidles down to my stomach, and slumber similarly sidles its way into my face and makes it relax. I

Saqi Books
26 Westbourne Grove
London W2 5RH
United Kingdom

I wish to be kept informed of your new publications and events

Subjects in which I have a special interest

☐ Art & Architecture ☐ History ☐ Politics ☐ Anthropology

☐ Women's Studies ☐ Fiction ☐ Poetry ☐ Languages

Other interests: ....

Name ....

Address ....

....

Postcode .... Country ....

E-mail ....

Your requests can also be sent by e-mail to: saqibooks@dial.pipex.com dream of sunny Mondays. Will this baby also be born on 15 of next May? Will it be a Monday again? Will it be room 401? Will it be afternoon?

The doors always open with a bang, and I'm soon aroused from my slumbers. Slowly I get out of bed and open my arms to give the little boy a hug. Shehab al-Din rushes towards me, Dunyazad runs behind him like a shadow, and behind her comes another tiny child with no visible features. Arms all intertwine around my neck. As Shehab al-Din opens his arms to me, my arm only embraces one thin body; the rest of the space I fill with longing. I offer him the life of the new being who will come from afar, and ever generous he allows me to plant a warm kiss on his forehead, a kiss that for now is only received by the air in my room. His tiny face receives that kiss now and stores it away for the days ahead. As Shehab al-Din slips away, the cluster of three children dissolves. Dunyazad flies off through the corridors and walls of the house. I remember when Shehab al-Din realized she had become a star in the sky and insisted on staying on his balcony every evening. The third child returns to its original resting place to wait . . .

Shehab al-Din undresses in his room. When he sees I'm feeling depressed, he gives me a kiss between the eyes. 'How much do you love me?' he asks. And without pausing for an answer he goes on, 'More than the whole world?'

Shehab al-Din Loves Salma

We were sitting at either end of the dining table. He was at the far left drawing, and I was writing at the other end.

Suddenly he looked up, a bit shy, but with a crafty smile as well. 'Mama,' he said softly, 'I saw a pretty girl today.'

Shehab? Four years old? I let my pen drop. 'What's her name?' I asked, beams of sheer joy radiating from my eyes,

He didn't reply. I went back to my writing, but was totally distracted. He carried on colouring, doing a drawing of himself: one big circle, with smaller ones in the middle for mouth and eyes, then an even bigger one for a fat body with two circular legs hanging down from it.

'Her name's Salma,' he tells me after a pause.

A smile from me and one back from him, a smile as tender as the memory of Salma's face that loomed in the space between us.

'Salma?' (I have a friend of that name.)

'Yes, I've just remembered.' (Perhaps he never forgot either.)

'Have you talked to her?'

'No!' he replies with obvious exasperation. This time he's drawing a prehistoric lizard, then a dinosaur . . .

I suppress the urge to ask more questions and decide to wait till he tells me more. Is she in the same class? When did he first notice her? What was she wearing? Is her hair black like mine? Why hasn't he spoken to her? Is she a nice girl or is she bad?

'When I woke up, I saw her standing there in front of me (so he saw her during nap time).

Love at first sight. He must have seen her in a dream, or else imagined that her face was a dream. Shehab al-Din is in love with Salma without even realizing it.

'Mama, I love Salma.'

So he does realize. I rush from one end of the table to the other and give him a hug. I decide to play the game through to the end. His little boy's heart is tired; he has to wait two more days before seeing her again.

He tries to wriggle his way out of my hug, but I hold him even tighter, as if in one final craving to possess him. Finally he struggles free. Four years old, and his heart is burdened by the lovely image of Salma.

Finally out of my clutches he seems surprised that I'm

laughing happily and thinks I'm making fun of him. He looks a bit embarrassed too.

'I'm going to marry you, Mama.'

Not a bad way of dealing with very precocious guilt-feelings. He's not going to leave me for another woman just yet.

'I'm already married to Daddy, my love.'

Joyous relief envelops his expression. The whole atmosphere clears, imbued with the scent of clouds that roll away after a heavy seasonal downpour.

I've decided: next Sunday I'm going to pick him up at kindergarten and ask him to point her out to me.

'There are two Salmas in the class,' he says, as though reading my very thoughts.

'Two Salmas?'

'Yes, there's pretty Salma and ugly Salma!'

'Which one do you love?'

'Pretty Salma.'

'You should talk to her.'

He's embarrassed. 'I don't know . . .!'

This boy's just like his father. I remembered I had to wait six months before he would admit he was in love with me and then another six months before he made up his mind to visit our house. I remembered too that the first present he gave me was a toy – typical of the romantic ideas of nineties lovers with their addiction to cartoons!

'You should choose a toy to give her.'

He stopped colouring. The idea obviously appealed to him. Jumping up from his chair he grabbed my hand and hurried me to his room. His toys were all over the floor, on his bed and on top of the cupboard. First he chose an expensive toy, a piano. This child's a romantic . . . not like his father, but then he doesn't really like the piano in any case.

'That's a big toy, Buba!'

He threw it on his bed. I was taken aback.

'What am I going to choose?'

I had forgotten that Shehab is a Gemini and chided myself. It was too late now; we were firmly into the possible and impossible choice phase. Rejected toys were all thrown on the bed; this one's big, this one's small; I like this one; this one's a present from Uncle K.; girls won't like this one . . .

'Mama, what do girls like to play with?'

An obvious question, one I'd never asked myself. Since Dunyazad I've never even thought I'd have another girl, or that I would buy her cotton dolls of the most expensive kinds made of plastic with proper skin colour.

'Dolls, small animals, musical toys.'

To make it easier for him to choose, I went through all the toys in his room. But it wasn't easy. At first he decided on a small doll called Karim, then he changed his mind and decided to give her a big doll in green clothes that looked like an Eskimo; then a wooden soldier, then a train, then a police car, then a box of blocks, and finally nothing at all.

'Talk to her first. If she's nice, you can buy her a present.'

'Do you mean she's not nice, Mama?' and he starts crying.

Bad move on my part. 'I didn't say that, darling,' I respond.

'You did!'

Not a bad way of bringing this procession of gift possibilities to an end and moving on to others yet more complex.

'I'm just going to play with boys.'

A third possibility, one that provided a radical solution to the entire issue but still made me feel guilty. Now I've given the boy a complex, I thought, as I gave him a hug and he tried angrily to get away.

I spent half the night looking for the right toy for Salma and the other half trying to get her lovely apparition out of my son's mind. He paces round and round the house, while I make valiant but useless efforts to divert his attention. Sometimes she's pretty and not nice, then she's pretty and nice; sometimes he's going to buy her a cookie, then he's turning his back on her in class as though she's his sworn enemy.

By now Salma must be asleep in her own little bed. When

she smiles, her teeth probably aren't straight; when Shehab sees her smile, he'll change his mind and stop thinking she's the prettiest girl in the class. A nice hot bath will calm him down, and then I'll tell him the story of Jamil the elephant and Abdel Fattah the crocodile. Just as he's closing his eyes on the image of Salma, I must remind him of where we're going tomorrow; to the zoo, with the pony doing the rounds of the elephant, camel, and horses. But tomorrow's trip doesn't erase the image completely. In the middle of the night I'm aware of him fidgeting as he remembers the tiny piano. I shake him a bit, and he gives me a hug. There, in a heady trance, are implanted between us images of first love.

Pregnancy Tests

'You should have another baby,' I was told.

Dunyazad's image has been erased from my memory. All that's left are two colours: blue for her face and white for her shroud. Fairly soon there'll just be a vague memory of a touch of blue, the pyramid-shaped mouth and closed eyes like all other mouths and eyes.

To keep the memory fresh, you have to really live a death story and feel a genuine desire to write it. You have to look at the face of a child strangled inside the womb to realize that friends' words and relatives' tears are all utterly absurd. So Dunyazad really died twice: the first time was six months ago when she decided to die so tragically; the second came a few days ago when she told me I was going to have another daughter who wouldn't look like her (would she live this time?). With that she died all over again.

I told myself I don't make babies this way based on a nocturnal decision; they're made in rare moments of love-making. When I can clearly make out two distinct lines on the pregnancy test, I realize I've gone beyond the uncertain stage and will complete the full nine-month term. Two lines (you're carrying 'a drop of sperm' from the mingled blood of the two of you).

That was a while ago. Now I make babies using simple arithmetic: on the fourteenth day I wait for a tiny ovary to receive the first signs of existence. Every night after the fourteenth I wait and open my body pores to receive. When the night-time regime comes to an end, a single question turns round and round in my mind . . . has it actually happened?

First I carry a drop of sperm, then a 'clot of blood'.

The first pregnancy test is in Paris; a hundred French francs. Early in the morning two pointers indicate that I'm carrying 'the first of my six children'. I send my mother a picture of a European baby and advise her to buy a cot with four sides and bars. I come home with a round stomach. A large family gathering is there at the airport to welcome me home in joyous anticipation. That's how Shehab al-Din came into the world. I'd passed my first pregnancy test.

The second pregnancy test is in Cairo; the price is cheap. My happiness is only matched by a real worry that I may give birth to a second boy. This time I long for the image of a little girl with plaits down her back and a little blue apron. I buy some sweet little clothes for her, all embroidered with tiny coloured roses, and get a bed ready for her tiny little body. I see an image of her body on the screen; later from the confines of my bed I see her dead, in a room too small for death.

The third pregnancy test is also in Cairo; the price has gone up a pound. Two pointers again. I swallow my regrets and walk hesitantly down the corridor to the dustbin, open it without looking, and throw the third test in. So now I'm going to have another baby and put an end to all my anxieties. Between the two pregnancy tests a year goes by, and the old fantasies come rushing back. A tiny baby with skin like velvet, a face with twinkling eyes . . . a replacement baby, someone who will one day read those very words and hate me.

On all three evenings I cried. Inside me I am carrying another life; faced with the new arrival I feel at once scared and grateful. Sorrow is part of the logic of things too, but the regret I feel the third time is far beyond any kind of fear or yearning. This time I have my own life in my hands as well. What if I have to run the risk of sudden death? What if there are no advanced indications as happened in Dunyazad's case? All signs indicate that a curse has taken possession of my body. After today I can give no more. Just one son, it decrees; whatever follows thereafter to the grave returns.

The dream of six children is now one short; a child, yet unborn, and there was none other like him.

I'm producing a third child; I've been carrying a drop of sperm, then a clot of blood. I see his pictures on the screen and love him as I should, and yet I don't love him as I should. He may actually come but, if this attempt fails, I may need a fourth pregnancy test.

It's not enough that I have to stop bursting into tears every time I set eyes on a five-month-old baby; in addition I have to control my overwhelming urge to kiss the baby as well.

If It's to Be a Girl

On the telephone the doctor's voice sounds soothing. There's a tense pause. 'I spotted you at the last Nasr Abu Zayd meeting,' I said, once we'd decided to fill the void.[1] 'Oh yes,' he replied, 'I try to go from time to time.' Before sympathy and welcome flagged I quickly put in my request: 'I'd like to see the report on Dunyazad's birth.' 'Who?' he asks. 'I'd like to see the medical report on my last delivery. I'm going on a trip soon.' 'Of course, of course,' he replied. 'It's all stored in the computer.' That makes me feel happier. There are other details too; they must be stored inside it somewhere. I won't understand what they mean, but other

---

1. Nasr Abu Zayd: a prominent Egyptian intellectual and university professor who, having written a work entitled *Critique of Religious Discourse* (Cairo, 1992), was declared a heretic. Subsequently his wife was divorced from him against her will by court action. They both now live in Leiden, Holland.

people, doctors and specialists, will. 'I saw you on television last week.' He's a fertility specialist. This time I wasn't lying; I did see him, talking in that same gentle voice about treatment possibilities; he had a tie on and was trying not to blink as much as usual. Just at that moment I remembered that this doctor of mine doesn't eat meat; he's a vegetarian. I hated lying to that gentle voice of his by pretending to be going away on a trip, but at any rate I was going somewhere.

Yet another doctor's clinic. His name's Sherif, a popular one for boys when we were young. There are pictures on the wall, all of them European women; the children look like coloured plastic dolls, with blonde hair, blue eyes, and rosy mouths. The mothers' breasts are tiny and soft where they touch the tiny soft cheek. Under one picture sits a fat woman; she's not pregnant but shows signs of childbirth – at least ten by the look of things. She's wearing a long, black head-scarf reaching down to the midpoint of her black galabiya; her withering glances target faces, empty seats, and the door left ajar. Under another picture sit a man and his wife, both of them tall as pharaonic statues, with broad shoulders, long necks, and silent heads. His face breaks into a smile when a little child gets up and asks his weary mother for a cup of water. I just sit there, carrying the baby inside me and waiting. The appointment is for eight in the evening, and it's now eight thirty. The doctor is in the examination room with a beautiful girl whose stomach is small and rounded; it's her first pregnancy. This is my third, and I'm waiting.

The nurse gestures me to follow her. In a small room connected to the doctor's office she takes my blood pressure and checks my weight. Then, like a small sacrificial animal prepared ahead of time, I am sent to the bathroom to do a new test.

My husband waits silently outside.

By now I recognize the usual bathroom features. I remember that in the first doctor's office the basin was different. Everything here is different. There may be less of a crowd, the walls look whiter, and there are only two nurses. The doctor has a boy's name, and people are odd. Everything's rejecting me. My first instinct after a couple of seconds' thought is to grab my husband's hand and head for the street, but after further thought I decide we will wait and see.

I no longer had a clear recollection of room 401 in the old hospital. The picture was dark, and the drawn curtains made it even more so. Now, whenever I looked up at the sky, Dunyazad's features started to fade, to be replaced by a feeling of compassion. I couldn't even imagine crossing the hospital threshold on a future visit. When I'd walked in some months ago, the security man stared at me inquisitively, maybe even sympathetically. That look left an outline on my back, and I'm determined that next time it won't happen; with a new birth our looks will never cross again.

Another gesture from the silent nurse, telling me to go in. The doctor's room is quiet; on either side of the large office there's a door. A computer takes up some space (I wonder what it's going to record this time).

My husband and I sat facing each other. As long as the doctor wasn't there, he let himself look nervous, but in the doctor's presence he was determined to control himself. Plucking up my courage I stared at the floor for a while; the quiet in the room was only slightly disturbed by the hum of the air-conditioner. At last the doctor came in and sat down; he had a child's smile to go with his name. As he looked at us, his smile lost some of its dazzle. I started talking. All I can remember now is the tremble in my voice and my overwhelming desire to burst into tears in front of him. It was as though I was complaining because they had all failed to save my daughter, or else I was begging him to save this new baby on the way, as though it were dead . . . dead. At this point my husband noticed I wasn't making any sense. He tried to find words that were more scientifically appropriate and finished the whole story.

By now the doctor wasn't smiling any more. His

expression had changed to one of profound sympathy and concealed apprehension; the sense of helplessness must have affected him too. He started asking for other details. I told him I'd asked my first doctor for a report. I begged this doctor not to tell the other one anything; in the long run he was the family doctor. I felt guilty; I'd never lied to my own doctor before, but now here I was betraying him by consulting another one!

Doctor Sherif speaks English, German, and French fluently. He's about forty-eight years old, wears glasses, and doesn't have a moustache. He has lived in Germany for several years. Every so often, he says 'Madam,' as if to lend his remarks a certain musical quality – something normal doctors don't do. He is very gentle, neat, and affectionate. Women fall in love with him at first glance, and husbands feel relaxed about him because he doesn't look like a Don Juan type. He's tall, and always leans forward slightly when he asks you to step into the examination room. With the nurse helping, he is extremely competent at his job. His sentences are usually short; words come tumbling out, interspersed with English medical terms that I picked up during my two previous pregnancies. That's why I seemed like a cultured woman; if I had not told him that I speak French and read books in it on childhood and birth, he would have tried talking to me in German as well.

We went through one of the two doors into the small examination room where there was a screen and bed. The nurse put some oily substance on my stomach; it smelled nice. The doctor placed a small black instrument on my stomach. The image of my womb appeared on the screen; with a press of the magnifying button I can see a tiny point attached to the black cavity and pulsating rhythmically. That's the foetus at ten weeks. 'Everything's fine,' the doctor said. 'You'll need some tests.'

When I rejoined my husband in the office, I was still managing to hold back my tears. He looked pale; his expression still bore traces of the story we'd told the doctor. By way of reassurance I gave him a feeble smile. I didn't feel my usual sense of pride at carrying a new baby. I sat bolt upright on the chair in front of him and looked away. 'What a lovely desk this is,' we said softly, 'it must be oak.' The doctor sat down at his desk and recorded his observations on a thick form divided into columns. He explained everything he was writing down and gave us a copy; we were to keep it and bring it with us every time we came for an examination so as to have a complete report. Everything is systematically recorded by date.

He had pointed at the screen. 'There's the placenta,' he said.

We walked side by side along the narrow street which was

crammed with large cars. I had confidence in this new doctor and wanted to impress my husband. 'He has a special device,' I said. 'During the delivery he puts it on your stomach to get data on the baby's condition and the intensity of the contractions. Everything . . . so there won't be another death.' Actually I wasn't fully convinced that such a thing was possible. So that was the placenta! If it becomes detached, the foetus dies within two minutes. As we crossed the street, he gave me a pat on the shoulder. We decided to walk home. At night the air smelled fresh, and there were few people on the streets. Inside my womb branches of a new tree were growing rapidly. Now I remembered that during the examination the doctor had explained to me that this technology could not prevent death. Even so, I swallowed his words of warning and put on an act to convince my husband that all was well. 'Suppose it's a girl,' I asked cheerfully. 'What are we going to call her?'

Turning Point

In just a few months I'd managed to write a new book, quit
my civil service job, have rows with several friends, smoke
the sixth cigarette of my life, and decide to have this third
baby that was now moving around inside me. I'd started
squabbling over trifles, almost knocked a man down on a
main road with my car, purchased lots of things, and hired
a new maid. I'd thrown a couple of receptions for friends,
and planted a new flowerbed on the balcony. I'd helped my
husband sell the family house and seen Shehab al-Din
through his first love experience and the process of waking
up at seven to go to school. As usual I'd avoided talking to
neighbours, but shown just how bored I felt by complaining
to the new doorman who never cleans the car properly and
to our new maid who manages to break the water tap in the
basin every time she uses it. I lost my temper with my

mother-in-law who keeps asking questions about everything and even with my husband when he started patting my behind every morning before anyone had washed their face or teeth.

Every day I concentrate on particular details and eliminate others from my calculations. I observe closely the way blood pulses through the veins on either side of my forehead and imagine that I have leukemia (so is that disease now coursing through the foetus of this third child that I'm expecting with no real enthusiasm? What if I really do have leukemia?).

Now I've started annoying my husband. He stayed away from the house for two nights, then came back. He handed me a long letter. With a gentle breeze wafting through the window I read it and burst into tears. So I still have tender feelings about things . . . even though by now I have protruding jaw and teeth. Images of Dracula or some other vampire (I don't remember which) manage to stifle some of the tears still lurking inside me. I feel scared and look behind me. There on the wall is an American horror movie.

Images from the movie: husband approaches wife. She doesn't even see him; she's busy sewing a short dress for her daughter. He sinks his voracious canines into her neck. The beautiful wife is transformed into a white, bloodless spectre.

Other possible images: the wife sinks her teeth into the neck of her daughter who can't cry out for help because the castle is completely cut off from the world and ghosts frolic in the back garden.

Scenes from another movie: ghosts don't copulate, but they don't get bored either. They can rip off veils, hover over haunted castles, and sing plaintively at dead of night.

So I can feel bored, I can raise hell with friends who offer me cigarettes with questionable substances, I can think of horror movies without being really scared, and every morning I can get Shehab al-Din ready for school by myself. I can also be recalcitrant, lackadaisical, and assertive; and I can be involved in life decisions without getting all fluttery and teary-eyed. Even when I'm taken unawares by a passing reference on some results to the number 15 or to Monday – reviving memories as painful as a pointed dagger, even then I can still hold back my tears; lastly I can feel really bored. So then, everything is permitted, everything is actually unimportant. To finish the page I write another line. Then I slide my feet into black slippers, turn out the light with a theatrical gesture, and slip into bed beside my sleeping husband. I don't listen to his breathing or mine. Tomorrow for sure we'll wake up to some fresh tedium.

'This is a turning point,' people will say. In a vast, more or less circular firmament of other points, spinning in memory orbits that record just a little. Like molecules of galaxies that vanish once they disintegrate; numerous transition points at multiple phases in their brief life.

The universe gives a yawn. From its open mouth emerge times, faces, a few smells, and forgotten images that follow their own zigzag paths to infinity. People also say, 'Everything happens according to a plan.'

How strange life's byways are, guiding none but the sightless.

A turning point at the cusp of death. Afterwards you can't find your way by sight alone. You close your eyes, open your arms wide, and spin in the galaxy you've designed, hoping to find the way. And, if you do, they say, 'a turning point'.

This is the end of writing.

Two weeks later a doctor's appointment.

I have a new friend I call Ula because she's nice too.

In the face of my old friend I have shut a door that has been open for years. By now I've lost all sense of her existence and she's forgotten how to get to my house, so I no longer give her a name.

I still find comfort in the ever outstretched arms of Shehab al-Din.

I'm still writing, although I've claimed it's the end of writing.

One friend dies, another leaves, still another fades away amid life's repetitive details. Some friends I don't write to because they're around; others I don't write to because they're stingy. I still dream of six sons; one son is enveloped by the spectre of death wherever he is. So what remains of my stars and galaxies as they orbit in the spaces of my personal history?

I am not giving my husband a name either. He has gentle eyes, a face with protruding cheeks like statues of ancient gods, and a fine body. Sometimes we quarrel, but only rarely does he raise his voice. A few weeks ago when he left the house because I . . . he came home and scolded me in French. I burst into tears. I loved him and didn't blame him; after all he's also Dunyazad's and Shehab al-Din's father.

It's a winter night; with it come dark thoughts.

Even so I resubmit my calculations to the gods of time as yet unborn.

The face of my old friend comes leaping through the windowpane, but I chase it away with a slight toss of the head. In its place I put a picture of Judas, so now I can contemplate the picture and the philosophy of history.

This is an ending appropriate for a postponed moment of mourning. I am writing Dunyazad, invoking the letters of her name to help me forget. Her round face and closed eyes hover over my head and follow a recognized orbit. Once in a while the eclipse affords her an incandescent glow. With her I go back, a child with no plaits, orbiting and drawing boundaries between what comes before her and what comes after. Beyond her lie spheres where still other faces collide, till they too settle into their preordained orbit.

A final moment of mourning. To all those who have fallen down the well of transition and died.

Cairo, 18 May–15 October 1995

Postface

The title of May Telmissany's remarkable novel, *Dunyazad*, is a female name; one that inevitably draws the reader to a famous earlier tale of Indo-Persian provenance (whence the name itself) in which Dunyazad accompanies her sister on a dangerous mission. We are talking, of course, about the frame-story of the world's most famous collection of narrative, *The Thousand and One Nights*. Dunyazad is Shahrazad's sister, entrusted with the task of proposing to the all-powerful virgin-slaying King Shahrayar that her learned sister be permitted to tell both him and her some of her large repertoire of stories. Dunyazad thus serves as a catalyst, the instigator of the story-telling function that will divert the king from his deadly intentions and provide him, Dunyazad, and many generations of listeners and readers with a glorious collection of stories.

May Telmissany is an inheritor of that narrative tradition, and her 'Dunyazad' also serves as a catalyst, albeit of a different kind and in a quite different context. The novel opens with Dunyazad's appearance, but this very beginning subverts the normal logic of narrative by presenting the reader with a closure that consists of that most unchallengeable of realities, death. Dunyazad has been stillborn, and her tiny corpse has already been prepared for burial. Her life has ended before it has even begun. The narrator of these awful moments is a young Egyptian mother, and the scenario is a hospital room where she is recovering – at least physically – from the effects of a highly problematic delivery, the full circumstances of which she does not yet know. Dunyazad's end is also a beginning for a transformed and potentially traumatic future that slowly emerges. The mother–narrator tells of the stages of her slow and emotionally fraught recovery in a series of narratives, impressions, and dreams. These intimate glimpses into the things she comes up with in order to cope with deeply ingrained instincts of retrospection and evasion and to confront the awesome reality of her loss convey their message in a style that is at once simple and direct, and yet possessed of a poetry of its own; how disarming (and ancient) for example is the image of the young mother's distressed brother standing 'as forlorn as a disused well'.

The linkage of the mother to her baby, Dunyazad, is, of course, the central motif of this narrative, but the tragedy is one that envelops and involves a whole family. The mother's account, with its sense of devastating loss and its search for both a reconciliation with the past and a path into the future, is matched in emotional impact by that of her husband. His sadness at the terrible turn of events is combined with an equal concern for the health of his beloved wife and mother of their little son. On him falls the initial burden of making arrangements for the baby's burial, of deciding how and when to tell his wife the full story of what happened, and of contacting and calming the various relatives on both sides of the family, not the least of whom, of course, are the two grandmothers. The narrative reveals with disarming candour the incredible strains that the situation puts on everyone. With the initial phases in the recovery process over, the simple act of coping with the needs of everyday life remains a colossal burden. Friends are anxious to visit to express their sympathy, and from all sides – not least that of the grandmothers – comes the advice to have another baby as soon as possible. All of which raises for both partners the issue of love, sex, and procreation within a domestic atmosphere that is fraught with tearful memories of what has happened and anxious fantasies about what might happen next time. The stress on the young couple is intense; it is the wife–narrator who acknowledges the strain her husband is under by confessing that her moodiness and irrational behaviour drive him to such as state of distraction that for two days he stays away from the house.

The family also has a third member, Shehab al-Din, their first child who does not comprehend the enormous effect that the events all around him are having on his parents. How does one tell a little boy that his baby sister has gone forever without his ever having seen her? However, it is perhaps the routines through which the mother caters to her living child and, in particular, schedules the day around his kindergarten timetable that contribute most to the slow process of her recovery. This is particularly the case during the most affecting chapter in which the mother–narrator finds herself confronting her son's first stirrings of love for a little girl in his kindergarten class. As she guides him – somewhat stumblingly – through the complexities of gender differences and decision making, she finds herself calling on reserves of motherly attention that help to steer her and the narrative towards the uncertain future of another birth.

To the tensions already present in the life of this young, tragedy-struck family is added the strain caused among the members of the husband's family by what has become almost a ritual in the life of so many Egyptian middle-class families: a decision to give in to the temptations of big money and to sell the family house. The old home, with its exquisite workmanship, tree-lined garden, and host of memories, is already surrounded by multi-storey blocks of flats. The decision to sell the house (where the young couple spent their wedding night to the accompaniment of bulldozers), and the family's move to a gleaming new apartment, surrounded by other similarly gleaming apartments, is incorporated into the narrative to become a completely appropriate symbol of the aspirations and problems of Egyptian society, and especially its middle class, in recent decades. How crushing is the narrator's depiction in 'Window on the Waiting Period' of the sheer banality of life in this environment: the parked cars, the unemployed husbands, and the routine of sex, cigarettes, and newspapers in furniture-filled rooms shuttered against the sunlight.

Thus far, we have concentrated on the ways in which this narrative portrays this Egyptian family within its private and personal domain, an environment to which the narrator introduces us with considerable candour and subtlety. However, as readers we are also afforded glimpses of the outside world within which the narrator has operated in the past and which she now confronts as part of a gradual (and often painful) re-involvement with the public domain. In this process a primary role is given to her friend, Nora, a work-colleague within the civil service. When the head of personnel in their department intimates to Nora that her friend is about to be subject to disciplinary action, the two women meet to discuss the situation. Nora herself narrates her side of the picture, noting that, even though her friend and work-colleague has declared her steadfast intention of submitting her resignation, she – Nora – expects her to change her mind. But Dunyazad's mother does not change her mind. The reader is thus treated to a wonderful depiction of the fishbowl atmosphere in a typical civil service office, with bureaucrats looking on in amazement as she submits her resignation to the head of personnel and, in a gesture of the purest defiance, insists on giving it to the boss in person – without a word spoken. And, with that 'procedure' duly dispatched, she buys herself a new dress to celebrate.

As is evident from the above commentary, this novel is very deliberately focused on the concerns of the person, on family relationships and the tensions resulting from an unexpected tragedy, and even on the ways in which outside forces impinge upon the lives of the narrators, and especially the principal narrator, Dunyazad's mother. The broader outside world of Egyptian politics and large national and international issues is not the central topic or concern of this work, and yet the narrative does allude to them in subtle ways. One relative is said to have died a martyr, a reference, no doubt, to one of the series of conflicts with Israel that have punctuated recent Egyptian history. With reference to the man whose obituary and photograph in the newspaper stir up so many vivid memories, we learn of a period of imprisonments and torture, a reference that will take every Egyptian reader back to the problematic era of the late 1950s and 1960s when, to quote any number of commentators, Egypt (and much of the Arab world) awoke from its post-revolutionary euphoria to find itself enclosed in a secret-police prison. In a much more specific and recent reference, the mother of Dunyazad reveals feelings about the recent dominance of popular Islamic movements over the lives and freedom of expression of Egypt's intellectuals by noting that she had spotted one of her obstetricians at a meeting held in support of Nasr Abu Zayd, the prominent critic of religious discourse and professor at the University of Cairo currently forced to live in exile in Holland.

Thus far, I have discussed the text of *Dunyazad* as a novel, the designation that May Telmissany herself provides. The author's very conscious awareness of recent trends in novel writing, and most especially the close attention to matters of style and levels of discourse, certainly justify such a mode of analysis. *Dunyazad* is indeed a remarkable narrative and, by virtue of both its treatment

93

of subject matter and the language in which it is couched, a major addition to the library of fiction penned by Arab women. As I have noted elsewhere, a primary role of Arab women writers since the 1950s has been to open up for fictional treatment a large societal space that male writers have been unable (and perhaps also unwilling) to explore: the complexities of family relationships and especially of gender differences. With the writings of Layla Ba'albaki, Ghadah Samman, and Hanan al-Shaykh, to provide just a few of the more famous names, the creative fictional space of all writers, male and female, has been enlarged – at least for those with the courage and insight to explore its many dimensions with the necessary insight and artistry.

That said, the narrator of *Dunyazad* indulges in several meta-fictional gestures, noting that she spends her time writing and that she has been questioned about the precise meaning of the title of a previous short story collection, 'Repetitive Sculptures' ('*Naht mutakarrir*'). That is in fact the title of May Telmissany's first collection, and so, utilizing the notions of Philippe Lejeune regarding the autobiographical pact, we can establish a linkage between the person whose name appears on the cover, the narrator (one of the narrators) of the work itself, and the first-person character whose actions and emotions are depicted within the text itself. The work thus identifies itself as one of those '*mémoires de la Méditerranée*', to cite the name of the European project within which *Dunyazad* is being translated and published. As part of that project and process, the translators of *Dunyazad* into six European languages gathered at the School of Translators in Toledo in July 1999 and worked with the author herself on the text and its translations. For two days we listened as she read her text out loud, page by page, chapter by chapter; after which we discussed many of the inner meanings and allusions in the text, often discovering through her insights hidden possibilities of meaning and delicious ambiguities that are bound to be the consequence of the process of transferring texts from one culture to another and, in this case, to a plurality of others. During these sessions the author's extreme awareness of the stylistic features of her own discourse and the breadth of her own readings in fiction were clearly evident; all of which have made me determined to make every effort to reflect those features, to the extent possible, in the English version.

After two days of reading we came to the end of the work, and at the final page the author declared herself unable to read the final section out loud. And, with that emotional moment, the linkage of the narrative whose features we had been discussing in such detached terms to the living person of its author and primary narrator struck home with a tremendous impact. The writing of *Dunyazad* thus emerges as an act of courage and a quest for release from a tragedy of enormous proportions. It is both a document of powerful emotive force and an important contribution to modern Arabic fiction.

Roger Allen
Philadelphia, July 1999

SAQI MODERN FICTION

Ghazi Algosaibi

Seven

242 pp; Hb ISBN 0 86356 088 1

Mohamed Choukri

For Bread Alone

170 pp; Pb ISBN 0 86356 138 1

Streetwise

164 pp; Pb ISBN 0 86356 045 8

Moris Farhi

Children of the Rainbow

389 pp; ISBN 0 86356 059 8

Mai Ghoussoub

Leaving Beirut

188 pp; Pb ISBN 0 86356 090 3

Agop Hacikyan & Jean-Yves Soucy

A Summer Without Dawn

560 pp; Hb ISBN 0 86356 538 7

Tawfik al-Hakim

Maze of Justice

136 pp; Pb ISBN 0 86356 200 0

Amos Kenan

The Road to Ein Harod

116 pp; Pb ISBN 0 86356 002 4

Aamer Hussein

This Other Salt

202 pp; Pb ISBN 0 86356 364 3
Hb ISBN 0 86356 379 1

Hoops of Fire

FIFTY YEARS OF PAKISTANI WOMEN WRITING
175 pp; Pb ISBN 0 86356 039 3

Ismail Kadare

Broken April

216 pp; Hb ISBN 0 86356 908 0

Doruntine

180 pp; Hb ISBN 0 86356 171 3

Sahar Khalifeh

Wild Thorns

208 pp; Pb ISBN 0 86356 003 2

Nawal El-Saadawi

Love in the Kingdom of Oil

190 pp; Pb ISBN 0 86356 070 9;
Hb ISBN 0 86356 079 2

The Fall of the Imam

192 pp; Pb ISBN 0 86356 069 5

Memoirs of a Woman Doctor

102 pp; Pb ISBN 0 86356 076 8;

Two Women in One

124 pp; Pb ISBN 0 86356 026 1

Abdel Rahman al-Sharqawi

Egyptian Earth

252 pp; Pb ISBN 0 86356 261 2;
Hb ISBN 0 86356 326 0

May Telmissany

Dunyazad

96 pp; Pb ISBN 0 86356 340 6;
Hb ISBN 0 86356 552 2

Tahir Wattar

The Earthquake

184 pp; Pb ISBN 0 86356 339 2;
Hb ISBN 0 86356 944 7